THE
BOOK OF BEASTS
E. NESBIT

Illustrated by
Annabel Spenceley

Beehive Books

He happened to be building a palace when the news came, and he left all the bricks kicking about the floor for Nurse to clear up — but then the news was rather remarkable news. You see, there was a knock at the front door downstairs, and Lionel thought it was the man come to see about the gas which had not been allowed to be lighted since the day when Lionel made a swing by tying his skipping-rope to the gas-bracket.

And then, quite suddenly, Nurse came in, and said, "Master Lionel, dear, they've come to fetch you to go and be King."

Then she made haste to change his clothes and to wash his face and hands and brush his hair, and all the time she was doing it Lionel kept wriggling and fidgeting and saying, "Oh, don't, Nurse," and, "I'm sure my ears are quite clean," or, "Never mind my hair, it's all right," and, "That'll do."

"You're going on as if you was going to be an eel instead of a King," said Nurse.

The minute Nurse let go for a moment Lionel bolted off without waiting for his clean handkerchief, and in the drawing-room there were two very grave-looking gentlemen in red robes with fur, and gold coronets with velvet sticking up out of the middle like cream in very expensive jam tarts.

They bowed low to Lionel, and the gravest one said:

"Sire, your great-great-great-great-great-grandfather, the King of this country, is dead, and now you have got to come and be King."

"Yes, please, sir," said Lionel. "When does it begin?"

"You will be crowned this afternoon," said the grave gentleman who was not quite so grave-looking as the other.

"Would you like me to bring Nurse, or what time would you like me to be fetched, and hadn't I better put on my velvet suit with the lace collar?" said Lionel, who had often been out to tea.

"Your Nurse will be removed to the palace later. No, never mind about changing your suit; the royal robes will cover all that up."

The grave gentlemen led the way to a coach with eight white horses, which was drawn up in front of the house where Lionel lived. It was No.7, on the left-hand side of the street as you go up.

Lionel ran upstairs at the last minute, and he kissed Nurse and said: "Thank you for washing me. I wish I'd let you do the other ear. No — there's no time now. Give me a hanky. Good-bye, Nurse."

"Good-bye, ducky," said Nurse. "Be a good little King now, and say 'please' and 'thank you', and remember to pass the cake to the little girls, and don't have more than two helps of anything."

So off went Lionel to be made King. He had never expected to be King any more than you have, so it was all quite new to him — so new that he had never even thought of it. And as the coach went through the town he had to bite his tongue to be quite sure it was real, because if his tongue was real it showed he wasn't dreaming. Half an hour before he had been building with bricks in the nursery; and now — the streets were all fluttering with flags;

every window was crowded with people waving handkerchiefs and scattering flowers; there were scarlet soldiers everywhere along the pavements, and all the bells of all the churches were ringing like mad, and like a great song to the music of their ringing he heard thousands of people shouting, "Long live Lionel! Long live our little King!"

He was a little sorry at first that he had not put on his best clothes, but he soon forgot to think about that. If he had been a girl he would very likely have bothered about it the whole time.

As they went along, the grave gentlemen, who were the Chancellor and the Prime Minister, explained the things which Lionel did not understand.

"I thought we were a Republic," said Lionel. "I'm sure there hasn't been a King for some time."

"Sire, your great-great-great-great-great-grandfather's death happened when my grandfather was a little boy," said the Prime Minister, "and since then your loyal people have been saving up to buy you a crown — so much a week, you know, according to people's means — sixpence a week from those who have first-rate pocket money, down to a halfpenny a week from those who haven't so much. You know it's the rule that the crown must be paid for by the people."

"But hadn't my great-great-however-much-it-is-grandfather a crown?"

"Yes, but he sent it to be tinned over, for fear of vanity, and he had had all the jewels taken out, and sold them to buy books. He was a strange man; a very good King he was, but he had his faults — he was fond of books. Almost with his last breath he sent the crown to be tinned — and he never lived to pay the tinsmith's bill."

Here the Prime Minister wiped away a tear, and just then the carriage stopped and Lionel was taken out of the carriage to be crowned. Being crowned is much more tiring work than you would suppose, and by the time it was over, and Lionel had worn the royal robes for an hour or two and had had his hand kissed by everybody whose business it was to do it, he was quite worn out, and was very glad to get into the palace nursery.

Nurse was there, and tea was ready: seedy cake and plummy cake, and jam and hot buttered toast, and the prettiest china with red and gold and blue flowers on it, and real tea, and as many cups of it as you liked. After tea Lionel said:

"I think I should like a book. Will you get me one, Nurse?"

"Bless the child," said Nurse, "you don't suppose you've lost the use of your legs with just being a King? Run along, do, and get your books yourself."

So Lionel went down into the library. The Prime Minister and the Chancellor were there, and when Lionel came in they bowed very low, and were beginning to ask Lionel most politely what on earth he was coming bothering for now — when Lionel cried out:

"Oh, what a worldful of books! Are they yours?" ·

"They are yours, your Majesty," answered the Chancellor.

"They were the property of the late King, your great-great —"

"Yes I know," Lionel interrupted. "Well, I shall read them all. I love to read. I am so glad I learned to read."

"If I might venture to advise your Majesty," said the Prime Minister, "I should not read these books. Your great —"

"Yes?" said Lionel quickly.

"He was a very good King. Oh, yes, really a very superior King in his way, but he was a little — well, strange."

"Mad?" asked Lionel, cheerfully.

"No, no" — both the gentlemen were sincerely shocked. "Not mad; but if I may express it so, he was — er — too clever by half. And I should not like a little King of mine to have anything to do with his books."

Lionel looked puzzled.

"The fact is," the Chancellor went on, twisting his red beard in an agitated way, "your great —"

"Go on," said Lionel.

8

"Was called a wizard."

"But he wasn't?"

"Of course not — a most worthy King was your great —"

"I see."

"But I wouldn't touch his books."

9

"Just this one," cried Lionel, laying his hands on the cover of a great brown book that lay on the study table. It had gold patterns on the brown leather, and gold clasps with turquoises and rubies in the twists of them, and gold corners, so that the leather should not wear out too quickly.

"I *must* look at this one," Lionel said, for on the back in big letters he read: "the *Book of Beasts*."

The Chancellor said, "Don't be a silly little King."

But Lionel had got the gold clasps undone, and he opened the first page, and there was a beautiful Butterfly all red, and brown, and yellow, and blue, so beautifully painted that it looked as if it were alive.

"There," said Lionel, "isn't that lovely? Why —"

But as he spoke the beautiful Butterfly fluttered its many-coloured wings on the yellow old page of the book, and flew up and out of the window.

"Well!" said the Prime Minister, as soon as he could speak for the lump of wonder that had got into his throat and tried to choke him. "That's magic, that is."

But before he had spoken the King had turned the next page, and there was a shining bird complete and beautiful in every blue feather of him. Under him was written, 'Blue Bird of Paradise', and while the King gazed enchanted at the charming picture the Blue Bird fluttered his wings on the yellow page and spread them and flew out of the book.

Then the Prime Minister snatched the book away from the King and shut it up on the blank page where the bird had been, and put it on a very high shelf. And the Chancellor gave the

King a good shaking, and said:

"You're a naughty, disobedient little King," and was very angry indeed.

"I don't see that I've done any harm," said Lionel. He hated being shaken, as all boys do; he would much rather have been slapped.

"No harm?" said the Chancellor. "Ah — but what do you know about it? That's the question. How do you know what might have been on the next page — a snake or a worm, or a centipede or a revolutionist, or something like that."

"Well, I'm sorry if I've vexed you," said Lionel. "Come, let's kiss and be friends." So he kissed the Prime Minister, and they settled down for a nice quiet game of noughts and crosses, while the Chancellor went to add up his accounts.

But when Lionel was in bed he could not sleep for thinking of the book, and when the full moon was shining with all her might and light he got up and crept down to the library and climbed up and got the *Book of Beasts*.

He took it outside on to the terrace, where the moonlight was as bright as day, and he opened the book, and saw the empty pages with 'Butterfly' and 'Blue Bird of Paradise' underneath, and then he turned the next page. There was some sort of red thing sitting under a palm tree, and under it was written 'Dragon'. The Dragon did not move, and the King shut the book up rather quickly and went back to bed.

But the next day he wanted another look, so he got the book out into the garden, and when he undid the clasps with the rubies and turquoises, the book opened all by itself at the picture with 'Dragon' underneath, and the sun shone full on the page. And then, quite suddenly the great Red Dragon came out of the book, and spread vast scarlet wings and flew away across the garden to the far hills, and Lionel was left with the empty page before him, for the page was quite empty except for the green palm tree and the yellow desert, and the little streaks of red where the paint brush had gone outside the pencil line of the Red Dragon.

And then Lionel felt that he had indeed done it. He had not been King twenty-four hours, and already he had let loose a Red Dragon to worry his faithful subjects' lives out. And they had been saving up for so long to buy him a crown, and everything!

Lionel began to cry.

Then the Chancellor and the Prime Minister and the Nurse all came running to see what was the matter. And when they saw the book they understood, and the Chancellor said:

"You naughty little King! Put him to bed, Nurse, and let him think over what he's done."

"Perhaps, my Lord," said the Prime Minister, "we'd better first find out just exactly what he *has* done."

Then Lionel, in floods of tears, said:

"It's a Red Dragon, and it's gone flying away to the hills, and I *am* sorry, and, oh, do forgive me!"

But the Prime Minister and the Chancellor had other things to think of than forgiving Lionel. They hurried off to consult the police and see what could be done. Everyone did what they could. They sat on committees and stood on guard, and lay in wait for the Dragon, but he stayed up in the hills, and there was nothing more to be done. The faithful Nurse, meanwhile, did not neglect her duty. Perhaps she did more than anyone else, for she slapped the King and put him to bed without his tea, and when it got dark she would not give him a candle to read by.

"You are a naughty little King," she said, "and nobody will love you."

Next day the Dragon was still quiet, though the more poetic of Lionel's

14

subjects could see the redness of the Dragon shining through the green trees quite plainly. So Lionel put on his crown and sat on his throne and said he wanted to make some laws.

And I need hardly say that though the Prime Minister and the Chancellor and the Nurse might have the very poorest opinion of Lionel's private judgement, and might even slap him and send him to bed, the minute he got on his throne and set his crown on his head, he became infallible — which means that everything he said was right, and that he couldn't possibly make a mistake. So when he said:

''There is a law forbidding people to open books in schools or elsewhere'' — he had the support of at least half of his subjects, and the other half — the grown-up half — pretended to think he was quite right.

Then he made a law that everyone should always have enough to eat. And this pleased everyone except the ones who had always had too much.

And when several other nice laws were made and written down he went home and made mud-houses and was very happy. And he said to his Nurse:

''People will love me now I've made such a lot of pretty new laws for them.''

But Nurse said: ''Don't count your chickens, my dear. You haven't seen the last of the Dragon yet.''

Now the next day was a Saturday. And in the afternoon the Dragon suddenly swooped down upon the common in all his hideous redness, and carried off the Football Players, umpires, goal posts, football, and all.

Then the people were very angry indeed, and they said:

''We might as well be a Republic. After saving up all these years to get his crown, and everything!''

And wise people shook their heads and foretold a decline in the National

16

Love of Sport. And, indeed, football was not at all popular for some time afterwards.

Lionel did his best to be a good King during the week, and the people were beginning to forgive him for letting the Dragon out of the book. "After all," they said, "football is a dangerous game, and perhaps it is wise to discourage it."

Popular opinion held that the Football Players, being tough and hard, had disagreed with the Dragon so much that he had gone away to some place where they only play cats' cradle and games that do not make you hard and tough.

All the same, Parliament met on Saturday afternoon, a covenient time, when most of the Members would be free to attend, to consider the Dragon. But unfortunately the Dragon, who had only been asleep, woke up because it was Saturday, and he considered the Parliament, and afterwards there were not any Members left, so they tried to make a new Parliament, but being an MP had somehow grown as unpopular as football playing, and no one would consent to be elected, so they had to do without a Parliament. When the next Saturday came round everyone was a little nervous, but the Red Dragon was pretty quiet that day and only ate an Orphanage.

Lionel was very, very unhappy. He felt that it was his disobedience that had brought this trouble on the Parliament and Orphanage and the Football Players, and he felt that it was his duty to try and do something. The question was, what?

The Blue Bird that had come out of the book used to sing very nicely in the palace rose-garden, and the Butterfly was very tame, and would perch on his shoulder when he walked among the tall lilies: so Lionel saw that *all* the creatures in the *Book of Beasts* could not be wicked, like the Dragon, and he thought:

"Suppose I could get another beast out who would fight the Dragon?"

So he took the *Book of Beasts* out into the rose-garden and opened the page next to the one where the Dragon had been just a tiny bit to see what the name was. He could only see 'cora', but he felt the middle of the page swelling up thick with the creature that was trying to come out, and it was only by putting the book down and sitting on it suddenly very hard, that he managed to get it shut. Then he fastened the clasps with the rubies and turquoises in them and sent for the Chancellor, who had been ill on Saturday week, and so had not been eaten with the rest of the Parliament, and he said:

"What animal ends in 'cora'?"

The Chancellor answered:

"The Manticora, of course."

"What is he like?" asked the King.

"He is the sworn foe of Dragons," said the Chancellor. "He drinks their blood. He is yellow, with the body of a lion and the face of a man. I wish we had a few Manticoras here now. But the last died hundreds of years ago — worse luck!"

Then the King ran and opened the book at the page that had 'cora' on it, and there was the picture-Manticora, all yellow, with a lion's body and a man's face, just as the Chancellor had said. And under the picture was written, 'Manticora'.

And in a few minutes the Manticora came sleepily out of the book, rubbing its eyes with its hands and mewing piteously. It seemed very stupid, and when Lionel gave it a push and said, "Go along and fight the Dragon, do," it put its tail between its legs and ran away. It went and hid behind the Town Hall, and at night when the people were asleep it went round and ate all the pussycats in the town. And then it mewed more than ever. And on the Saturday morning, when people were a little timid about going out, because the Dragon had no regular hour for calling, the Manticora went up and down the streets and drank all the milk that was left in the cans at the doors for people's teas, and it ate the cans as well.

And just when it had finished the very last ha'porth, which was short measure, because the milkman's nerves were quite upset, the Red Dragon came down the street looking for the Manticora. It edged off when it saw him coming, for it was not at all the dragon-fighting kind; and, seeing no other door open, the poor, hunted creature took refuge in the General Post Office, and there the Dragon found it, trying to conceal itself among the ten o'clock mail. The Dragon fell on the Manticora at once and the mail was no defence. The mewings were heard all over the town. All the pussies and the milk the Manticora had had seemed to have strengthened its mew wonderfully. Then there was a sad silence, and presently the people whose windows looked that way saw the Dragon come walking down the steps of the General Post Office spitting fire and smoke, together with tufts of Manticora fur, and the

fragments of the registered letters. Things were growing very serious. However popular the King might have become during the week, the Dragon was sure to do something on Saturday to upset the people's loyalty.

The Dragon was a perfect nuisance for the whole of Saturday, except during the hour of noon, and then he had to rest under a tree or he would have caught fire from the heat of the sun. You see, he was very hot to begin with.

At last came a Saturday when the Dragon actually walked into the royal nursery and carried off the King's own pet Rocking-Horse. Then the King cried for six days, and on the seventh he was so tired that he had to stop. Then he heard the Blue Bird singing among the roses and saw the Butterfly fluttering among the lilies, and he said:

"Nurse, wipe my face, please. I am not going to cry any more."

23

Nurse washed his face, and told him not to be a silly little King. "Crying," said she, "never did anyone any good yet."

"I don't know," said the little King, "I seem to see better, and to hear better now that I've cried for a week. Now, Nurse, dear, I know I'm right, so kiss me in case I never come back. I *must* try if I can to save the people."

"Well, if you must, you must," said Nurse, "but don't tear your clothes or get your feet wet."

So off he went.

The Blue Bird sang more sweetly than ever, and the Butterfly shone more brightly, as Lionel once more carried the *Book of Beasts* out into the rose-garden, and opened it — very quickly, so that he might not be afraid and change his mind. The book fell open wide, almost in the middle, and there was written at the bottom of the page 'The Hippogriff', and before Lionel had time to see what the picture was, there was a fluttering of great wings and a stamping of hoofs, and a sweet, soft, friendly neighing; and there came out of the book a beautiful white horse with a long, long, white mane and a long, long, white tail, and he had great wings like swan's wings, and the softest, kindest eyes in the world, and he stood there among the roses.

The Hippogriff rubbed its silky-soft, milky-white nose against the little King's shoulder, and the little King thought: "But for the wings you are very like my poor, dear, lost Rocking-Horse." And the Blue-Bird's song was very loud and sweet.

Then suddenly the King saw coming through the sky the great straggling, sprawling shape of the Red Dragon. And he knew at once what he must do. He caught up the *Book of Beasts* and jumped on the back of the gentle, beautiful Hippogriff, and leaning down he whispered in the sharp white ear:

"Fly, dear Hippogriff, fly your very fastest to the Pebbly Waste."

And when the Dragon saw them start, he turned and flew after them, with his great wings flapping like clouds at sunset, and the Hippogriff's wide wings were snowy as clouds at the moon-rising.

When the people in the town saw the Dragon fly off after the Hippogriff and the King they all came out of their houses to look, and when they saw the two disappear they made up their minds to the worst, and began to think what would be worn for court mourning.

But the Dragon could not catch the Hippogriff. The red wings were bigger

than the white ones, but they were not so strong, and so the white-winged horse flew away and away and away, with the Dragon pursuing, till he reached the very middle of the Pebbly Waste.

Now, the Pebbly Waste is just like the parts of the seaside where there is no sand — all round, loose, shifting stones, and there is no grass there and no trees within a hundred miles of it.

Lionel jumped off the white horse's back in the very middle of the Pebbly Waste, and he hurriedly unclasped the *Book of Beasts* and laid it open on the pebbles. Then he clattered among the pebbles in his haste to get back on to his white horse, and had just jumped on when up came the Dragon. He was flying very feebly, and looking round everywhere for a tree, for it was just on the stroke of twelve, the sun was shining like a gold guinea in the blue sky, and there was not a tree for a hundred miles.

The white-winged horse flew round and round the Dragon as he writhed on the dry pebbles. He was getting very hot: indeed, parts of him had even begun to smoke. He knew that he must certainly catch fire in another minute unless he could get under a tree. He made a snatch with his red claws at the King and Hippogriff, but he was too feeble to reach them, and besides, he did not dare to over-exert himself for fear he should get any hotter.

It was then that he saw the *Book of Beasts* lying on the pebbles, open at the page with 'Dragon' written at the bottom. He looked again, and then, with one last squirm of rage, the Dragon wriggled himself back into the picture, and sat down under the palm tree, and the page was a little singed as he went in.

As soon as Lionel saw that the Dragon had really been obliged to go and sit under his own tree because it was the only tree there, he jumped off his horse and shut the book with a bang.

"Oh, hurrah!" he cried. "Now we really *have* done it."

And he clasped the book very tight with the turquoise and ruby clasps.

"Oh, my precious Hippogriff," he cried, "you are the bravest, dearest, most beautiful —"

"Hush," whispered the Hippogriff, modestly. "Don't you see that we are not alone?"

And indeed there was quite a crowd round them on the Pebbly Waste: the Prime Minister and the Parliament and the Football Players and the Orphanage and the Manticora and the Rocking-Horse, and indeed everyone who had been eaten by the Dragon. You see, it was impossible for the Dragon to take them into the book with him — it was a tight fit even for one Dragon, so, of course, he had to leave them outside.

They all got home somehow, and all lived happy ever after.

When the King asked the Manticora where he would like to live he begged to be allowed to go back into the book. "I do not care for public life," he said.

Of course he knew his way on to his own page, so there was no danger of his opening the book at the wrong page and letting out a Dragon or anything. So he got back into his picture, and has never come out since: that is why you will never see a Manticora as long as you live, except in a picture-book. And of course he left the pussies outside, because there was no room for them in the book — and the milk-cans too.

Then the Rocking-Horse begged to be allowed to go and live on the Hippogriff's page of the book. "I should like," he said, "to live somewhere where Dragons can't get at me."

So the beautiful, white-winged Hippogriff showed him the way in, and there he stayed till the King had him taken out for his great-great-great-great-grandchildren to play with.

As for the Hippogriff, he accepted the position of the King's Own Rocking-Horse — a situation left vacant by the retirement of the wooden one. And the Blue Bird and the Butterfly sing and flutter among the lilies and roses of the palace garden to this very day.

First published in 1899

This edition first published in Great Britain 1987 by
Beehive Books, an imprint of Macdonald & Company (Publishers) Limited,
Greater London House, Hampstead Road, London, NW1 7QX

A BPCC plc company

© **This edition Macdonald & Company (Publishers) Limited 1987**

Typeset by Angel Graphics, London. Origination by Scancraft, London.
Printed in Spain by Novograph, S.A., Madrid

British Library Cataloguing in Publication Data

Nesbit, E.
The book of beasts. —— (Nesbit picture book classics; 1).
I. Title II. Spenceley, Annabel III. Series
823'.8[J] PZ7

ISBN 0-356-13389-3